W9-COL-973

TEMPLETON GETS HIS WISH

GREG PIZZOLI

DISNEY • HYPERION Los Angeles New York

Templeton wanted his family to leave him alone.

His mom was grumpy.

His dad was cranky.

And his little brothers were
always taking his favorite toys.

But then . . .

Templeton had an idea.

He would wish them all away.

So he did something bad,

and got something good in return.

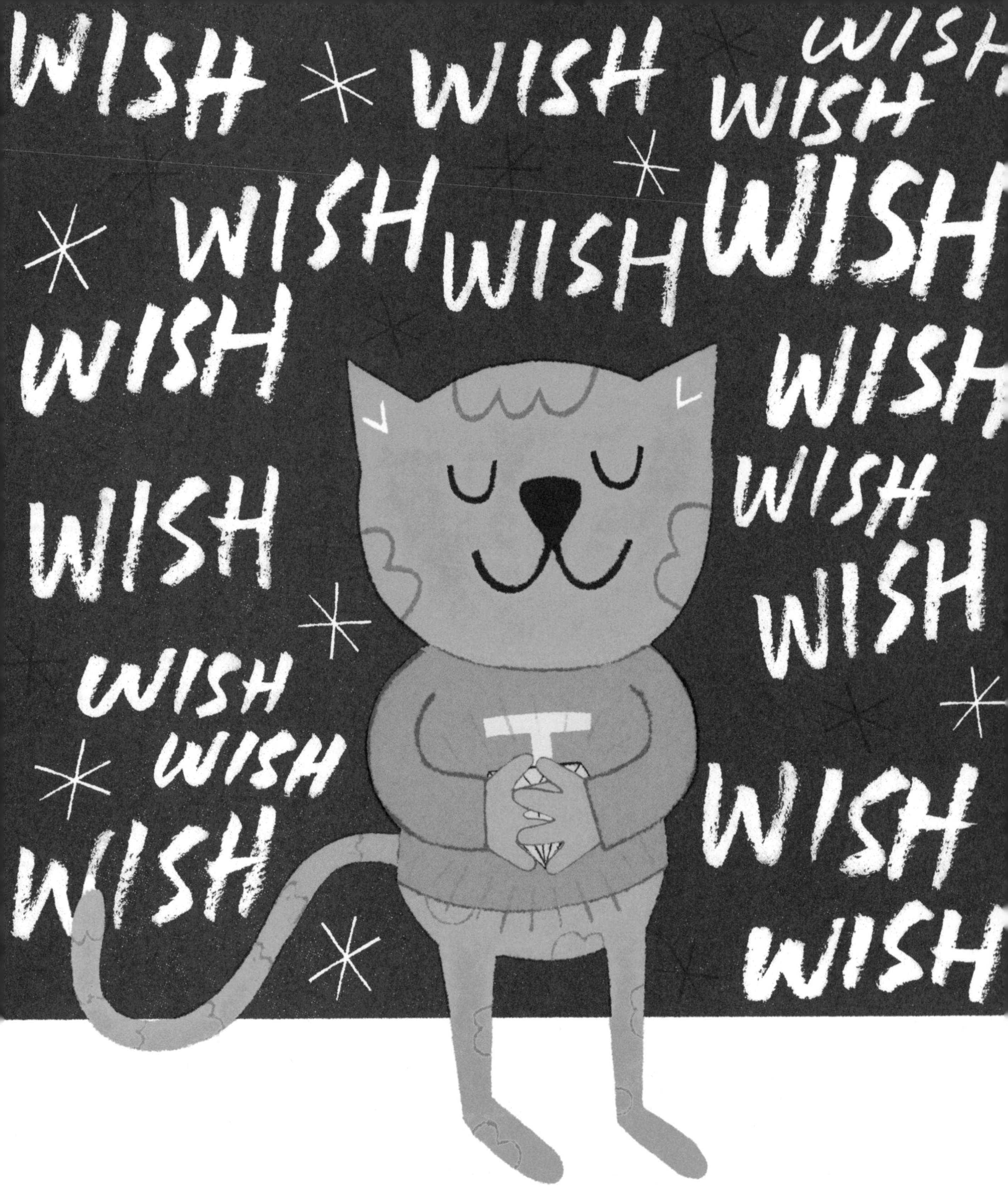

WISH WISH WISH
WISH
WISH WISH WISH
WISH
WISH
WISH
WISH
WISH
WISH
WISH
WISH
WISH
WISH

Then he wished on the magic diamond.

And Templeton got his wish.

His family was gone.

No more "Templeton, take a bath!"

No more "Templeton, clean this up!"

No more "Templeton, share your toys!"

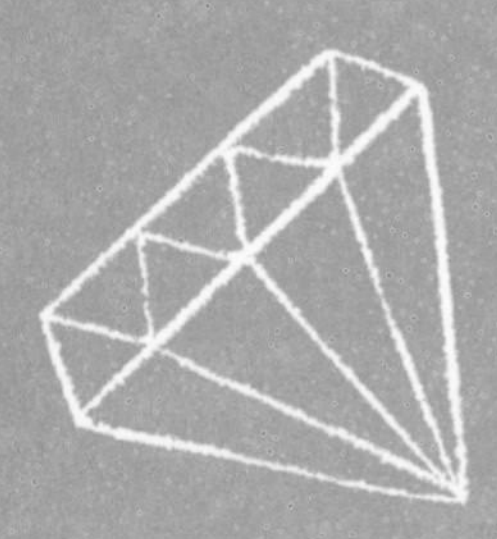

He was free.

Templeton played.

TEMPLETON

Templeton sang.

Templeton lounged.

Templeton did **NOT** clean up.

TEMPLETON
TEMPLETON
TEMPLETON

Templeton did NOT take a bath.

And Templeton did NOT have to share his toys with anyone at all.

But after a while, the house seemed really quiet.

And sometimes it was a little scary.

There was no one to play with.

And he was starting to think
he might need a bath after all.

Templeton was alone.

So Templeton wished that he had never wished his family away in the first place.

He wished things were back to the way they had been before he ever got the magic diamond.

And Templeton got his wish.

And his mom ran to him with
tears in her eyes and said,

"You need a bath!"

And his dad embraced him in
a big bear hug and whispered,

"Clean up this mess!"

And soon his brothers had taken ALL of his favorite toys.

Everything was back to normal.

Templeton had wished for his family . . .

TIME FOR BED, TEMPLETON!

And Templeton got his wish.

For my family

 Published by Disney • Hyperion, an imprint of Disney Book Group. For information address Disney • Hyperion, 125 West End Avenue, New York, New York 10023 • First Edition, May 2015 • 10 9 8 7 6 5 4 3 2 1 • H106-9333-5-15015 • Printed in Malaysia • Library of Congress Cataloging-in-Publication Data • Pizzoli, Greg, author, illustrator. • Templeton gets his wish / Greg Pizzoli.—First edition. • pages cm • Summary: "Templeton the cat makes a wish for his family to disappear, but quickly learns that being alone isn't as great as he had thought it would be"—Provided by publisher. • ISBN 978-1-4847-1274-0 — ISBN 1-4847-1274-9 • [1. Family life—Fiction. 2. Wishes—Fiction. 3. Cats—Fiction.] I. Title. • PZ7.P6898Te 2015 • [E]—dc23 2014017391 • Reinforced binding • Visit www.disneybooks.com